# Contents

Otter-Barry BOOKS

Lolo's Special Soup

One cold and rainy morning, Mama had to go out. So she dressed warmly and said to Lolo, "Be a good girl and listen to Gogo."

"Yes, Mama," said Lolo.

Gogo and Lolo watched Mama walk
into the cold and rain. Poor Mama!

When she disappeared down the road,
Gogo said, "Brrr, I'm going back to bed."

Lolo poured her favourite breakfast cereal
into a bowl, added some milk and gave it a
stir. And *that's* when she got her brilliant idea.

So, when she finished eating, she got out
a pot and looked in the fridge to see what
she could add to it. Ah, last night's leftovers
of rice and gravy! Lolo plopped the leftovers
into the pot and gave it a stir.

Then Lolo stood on a chair to peek
into the food cupboard.

Just then Gogo came into the kitchen.

"What are you doing?" asked Gogo.

"Making soup for Mama to have when
she comes home," said Lolo.

"What a lovely idea," said Gogo. "Let me help you." Gogo looked into the pot.

"What's that?" she asked.

"Leftovers," replied Lolo.

"That's a good way to start a soup," said Gogo, "but we need something else."

"I know. Bananas! Mama likes bananas," said Lolo.

"You don't put bananas in soup, Lolo," said Gogo. "What we need is a carrot."

While Gogo peeled and chopped a carrot,
Lolo went to the cupboard and came back
with a packet of ginger biscuits.

"Mama's mad about these," said Lolo,
"and they will make the soup very tasty."

Gogo giggled. "Oh, Lolo,
nobody puts biscuits
into soup. What we need
is a tin of tomatoes,
an onion and a pinch
of vegetable stock.

That's how you make soup!"

Gogo added tomatoes and vegetable stock
and Lolo stirred the pot.

Next, Gogo sliced an onion. Soon there were tears in her eyes.

"Eish!" gasped Gogo. "Onions make me cry. And crying makes my nose run. Please keep stirring while I go and blow my nose."

Lolo stirred and watched all the soupy things that Gogo had added go round and round. The only thing *she* had added were the leftovers. It wasn't fair! This was meant to be Lolo's special soup for Mama – not Gogo's!

So while Gogo was away, Lolo went back to the cupboard and found something special that she *knew* Mama absolutely loved. Quickly, she added it to the soup and gave it a stir.

When Gogo returned, she said, "Mmmm, now it's smelling like special soup!"

Gogo turned off the heat and said, "Now we'll warm it up just before your mama comes home."

While waiting for Mama to come home, Lolo went to her room and did some rainy-day things – she coloured in a picture and added stickers to the page. Then she looked at the rain pitter-patter against the window. Which raindrop would reach the bottom of the window first?

After lunch, Lolo crept into bed with Gogo for story-time. While Gogo read, Lolo fell asleep. The next thing she heard was Mama calling, "I'm home!"

Mama looked cold and tired.

"I'm starving!" said Mama, removing her wet coat. "What's that lovely smell?" she asked.

"Lolo's made soup for you," said Gogo.

"Oh, thank you, Lolo," said Mama. "That's just what I need to warm me up."

As soon as Mama had changed into dry clothes the soup was nice and hot, so they sat down to eat.

"Mmmm," said Mama, "this is delicious! What's making it taste so special?"

"I added vegetable stock," said Gogo.

"No," said Mama, "that's not what I'm tasting."

Lolo kept quiet. Gogo frowned.

"I'm tasting something yummy and sweet!" said Mama.

When the soup was finished, Mama stood up and said, "Now I've got something that I've been saving for a special occasion."

Mama went to the food cupboard and scratched around. But she couldn't find what she was looking for.

"Strange," said Mama. "I was saving three pieces of my favourite chocolate for a special occasion."

Lolo looked straight ahead, but she could feel Gogo staring at her.

"Lolo," asked Gogo, "what have you done with your mama's chocolate?"

 Lolo started to cry as she told Mama that she had added Mama's favourite chocolate to the soup.

But instead of being cross, Mama laughed. "So *that's* what has made your soup taste so special!"

Lolo looked up and wiped her tears.

"You know, Lolo darling," said Mama, "it was very thoughtful of you to make soup for me. What do you call it?"

"Lolo's Special Soup," said Lolo.

"Well, it really is the best soup I have ever tasted!" said Mama, giving her a hug.

"And *that's* as true as chocolate is sweet," chuckled Gogo, licking her lips.

Lolo's Scary Night

One dark windy night, Lolo woke up to

a scary sound. It went,

"*Ghorra-Ghorra!*"

Then it stopped and went,

"*Hoooaaah! Bwoooooo!*"

like some big, scary monster howling in

the wind.

Lolo's room was dark except for streaky shapes that shivered against the bedroom wall from a street light. Lolo pulled her duvet over her head. But she could still hear the sound – deeper and scarier this time.

Ghorra–Ghorra!
Hoooaaah!
Bwooooo!

Quickly, Lolo put on her slippers and dressing gown and ran to Mama's bedroom.

"Mama! Mama!" whispered Lolo. "Wake up!"

"What's the matter, Lolo?" asked Mama sleepily.

"Listen!" said Lolo. "There's a scary sound coming from somewhere."

Mama switched on her bedside lamp and listened.

"It's only the wind blowing through the wires outside," whispered Mama.

"No, not that!" whispered Lolo. "A *really* scary sound – like a monster."

"Well, you'd better climb into bed with me," whispered Mama.

"What did it sound like?" asked Mama.

Lolo went,

"Ghorra-Ghorra!
Hoooaaah!
Bwooooo!"

"That's the sound the nice Ghorra-Ghorra-Hoooaaah-Bwoooooo-Monster makes to chase away really bad monsters," said Mama.

"What does it look like?" whispered Lolo.

"It has big fluffy pink feet," whispered Mama.

"Like my slippers," said Lolo. "What else?"

"It's very round and covered in polka dots," whispered Mama.

"Like my dressing gown," said Lolo. "What else?"

"It has a puff-ball nose, bat wings and a curly-whirly tail," whispered Mama. "It's really sweet."

Then Lolo knew that Mama was making it all up! But she was already starting to fall asleep, so she didn't argue.

All was quiet –
only the wind blowing
through the wires. Lolo
slept with Mama's arms wrapped
around her. Then it happened again...

Ghorra-Ghorra!
Hoooaaah!
Bwoooooo!

This time the strange sound woke Mama.
"Ghorra-Ghorra! Hoooaaah! Bwoooooo!"
Mama tried sitting up. But her left arm
had gone dead from Lolo lying on it.

33

"Lolo! Lolo!" whispered Mama. "Wake up. This bed's too small for the two of us." Mama got Lolo out of bed and they tiptoed to Gogo's room.

"Climb in!" whispered Mama.

Lolo got in beside Gogo, leaving space for Mama to join her. No sooner had they settled down when...

"Ghorra-Ghorra! Hoooaaah! Bwoooooo!"

It was Gogo – snoring her head off!

Mama pulled Lolo close to her and giggled.

"It's not the Ghorra-Ghorra-Hoooaaah-Bwoooooo-Monster," whispered Mama. "It's the Snoring-Gogo-Monster!"

They both giggled until the bed shook. Gogo stirred and immediately stopped snoring.

Outside, the wind dropped.

At last all was quiet and Gogo, Mama and Lolo slept – as snug as three bugs in a rug.

Lolo's Snail Garden

Lolo's favourite teacher was Mr Penfold. He taught Life Skills and always had cool ideas. So when he set a garden project, everyone was excited – even the children who lived in homes that had no gardens.

"You can grow vegetables in a bin bag filled with soil," said Mr Penfold.

"My tata grows tomatoes in a tin can," added Zinzi.

"Yes," said Mr Penfold, "there are many ways to garden."

Mr Penfold showed them pictures of all kinds of gardens.

A garden in an old car tyre.

A seed garden in a bottle.

A garden against a wall.

An indoor garden.

So many ideas for making a garden.

Mr Penfold took them round the back
of the school where the Year 5s had started
a garden. The enclosed patch looked like
a forest of plants – beans, carrots, squash,
radishes and marog, an African spinach.

There were also some tall sunflowers with their sunny faces pointing up to the sun.

"See," said Mr Penfold, "if you take good care of a garden, it will take care of you."

Back in class, Mr Penfold handed out small packets of seeds to everyone. Some got carrot seeds, some got pumpkin seeds, others got dried beans and Lolo and the rest got tomato seeds.

Next, Mr Penfold opened his laptop and showed them how to germinate their seeds before putting the little seedlings into the earth.

It was simple, but it needed patience. And Lolo couldn't wait to get started.

At home, Gogo helped her set up a seed tray using a plastic container lined with paper towel.

"Now we must find a nice place in the sun for your seeds," said Gogo.

"No," said Lolo. "Mr Penfold told us that seeds must first grow in a dark place, like they do when they are under the ground. We must wait for the little thingies to push through the paper, then we can put them where they will get some sunlight."

"Now *you're* teaching me something," said Gogo, giving Lolo a squeeze.

Gogo found a shoe box that Lolo could keep her plastic tray of seeds in.

Every morning before going to school, Lolo peeped inside the shoe box to make sure the paper towel was damp – not wet, just nice and damp. And every night before going to bed she did the same.

After three days something amazing happened...

"Gogo! Mama! Come and look!" cried Lolo.

Lots of little shoots were sticking out of the damp paper towel.

"While you're at school I'll look for something you can plant them in," said Gogo.

That day, in Life Skills class, everyone had news about their seedlings. Some of it was sad news.

"Mine went all funny and started to smell," said Dana Rose.

"My beans didn't do *anything*," said Rhapelang. "They just got all wrinkled."

Mr Penfold gave them new seeds and encouraged them not to give up.

When Lolo arrived home that day, Gogo had found a perfect container for the seeds – an egg box. Lolo took it outside and carefully filled each cup with soft soil. Gogo helped her plant the seedlings into the egg-box cups.

Lolo placed the egg-box on the windowsill, where it caught the morning sun.

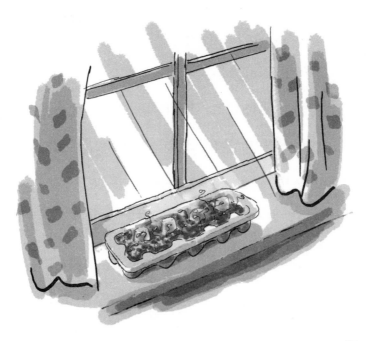

Days went by as Lolo looked after her seedlings. Then one day Gogo called out, "Lolo! Come quick! Look!"

Gogo pointed to the tiny leaves that had sprouted from the delicate stems. Gogo was very excited but Lolo said, "Those aren't the *true* leaves. Mr Penfold said we must wait for the *true* leaves before planting them in the garden."

"Ag! A leaf is a leaf!" grumbled Gogo, but Lolo showed her the worksheet that Mr Penfold had given them. It showed that the first two leaves are called *seed leaves*. You have to wait for the next leaves called *true leaves* to grow before planting them in the garden.

So they waited and waited.

Then, after two weeks, it happened!

"Gogo!" yelled Lolo. "Look! True leaves!"

And there, out of the stems of the seedlings, two true green leaves had sprouted. Now the seedlings were ready to be planted in the garden!

Gogo stood back to admire Lolo's garden. "Well done, Lolo!" she said.

Lolo felt very proud of her garden. Mr Penfold was right – it took care and a lot of patience to be a gardener.

When Mama came home, she took a photo
of Lolo's garden.

"Mmmm, I can't wait for your tomatoes to
grow," said Gogo. "I love cheese and tomato
sandwiches."

"I *luuuurve* tomatoes in salad," said Mama.

"I don't like tomatoes at all," said Lolo,
"but I luuuurve growing them!"

Lolo's tomato plants loved the sun and were growing beautifully.

Then one morning, when Lolo went to water her plants before going to school...

SNAILS!

During the night they had had a tomato-leaf party! Only stems were left.

Lolo shrieked, *"Mama! Gogo!"*

Gogo lifted her foot to squash a little snail.

"Wait, Gogo!" cried Lolo. She was thinking.

"But Lolo, they have eaten up your garden!" spluttered Gogo.

"I know," said Lolo thoughtfully. "But... I *think* I might like snails more than I like tomatoes!"

Gogo looked at Mama, then burst out laughing. That Lolo!

When Mr Penfold asked the children
to bring to class anything they'd managed
to grow,

Shane brought a squash,

Gift brought a bunch
of marog,

Cleo brought something
she'd forgotten to water,

Kay Lee brought two
hairy potatoes,

Dana Rose brought a
small, but very nice carrot,

Busi brought
garden-fresh radishes,

and Lolo?

Lolo brought six

very healthy-looking snails

in a shoe box!

Lolo's Holiday

"Lolo," said Gogo, "would you like to spend a holiday with me at Aunty Boni's?"

"Who's Aunty Boni?" asked Lolo.

"Aunty Boni is my cousin," said Gogo. "Her real name is Boniswa and she lives at the seaside, in a town called Kleinmond."

"It will be a nice holiday for you and Gogo," said Mama.

"We will go when school finishes this term," said Gogo.

On the last day of term, Miss Twala asked the children, "So what are you all doing during your holiday?"

Most of the children were staying at home. A few were going away. Miss Twala rolled down a map for the lucky ones to see where they would be going on holiday.

Felicity was taking a bus to the Eastern Cape.

Xoli was catching a train to Gauteng.

Thabo MacRobert was going overseas in an aeroplane.

Lolo wondered if she and Gogo might take an aeroplane to Kleinmond. But Miss Twala said that Kleinmond was not very far from Cape Town. There it was, on the map, next to the blue sea.

"You can go by car," said Miss Twala.

me and Gogo

Gogo's old friend, Mr Koza, offered to drive Lolo and Gogo to Kleinmond.

Mama helped Lolo pack her things. Then she tied two bright yellow ribbons in Lolo's hair.

"Now you look like a holiday girl," said Mama.

"Ready?" asked Gogo.

"Ready!" said Lolo.

Off they went in Mr Koza's old car that went *chug-chugging* along the highway, letting shiny new cars whizz by.

Gogo turned round and smiled at Lolo. "Don't worry, Lolo," she said. "We'll get there."

After a while, they turned off the highway
onto a steep road that went up, up, up
and down, down, down – all around the
mountainside, with a big sea down below.

Mr Koza whistled happily while his old car squeaked, rattled and went chug-a-lug.

Then it went *chug-a-lug-flap-flap*! Mr Koza stopped whistling. The old car had broken down!

They climbed out and Mr Koza opened
the bonnet, looked in and pulled out a
scruffy thing that looked like a big worn-out
rubber band.

"The fan belt has broken!" said Mr Koza.

"Eish!" sighed Gogo. "Does that mean that
your car can't go any further?"

"Yes," said Mr Koza.

Lolo bit her lip.

"Don't worry, Lolo," said Gogo. "We'll get
there... somehow."

"If I can find something that can work like a fan belt, we can be on our way," said Mr Koza.

"Like what?" asked Gogo.
"Like ribbons!" said Mr Koza, spotting Lolo's ribbons.

"But these are my holiday ribbons!" cried Lolo.

"Well, we are not going to have a holiday if we don't get to Kleinmond," explained Gogo.

So Lolo handed her lovely ribbons to Mr Koza, who twisted them into a strong band. Then he fitted it where the fan belt should go.

"Fingers crossed!" cried Mr Koza.

Lolo closed her eyes and made a wish.

Chug-chug... chug-a-lug-a-lug-a-lug.

The old car started!

"Jump in!" cried Mr Koza.

And off they went.

By late afternoon they arrived at
Aunty Boni's.

"I'll fetch you in a week's time," said
Mr Koza.

"Thank you," said Gogo.

"Thanks for your ribbons, Lolo.
They saved the day!" called Mr Koza as he
chug-a-lugged off in his old car.

"Now we can start our holiday!" sang
Gogo.

And what a holiday they had!

Lolo and Gogo paddled in the blue sea.

They walked on the mountainside.

And Lolo got new ribbons.

Oh, *what* a lot of fun they had at Aunty Boni's – they even laughed about Mr Koza's old car breaking down.

"It's a real rust bucket," laughed Gogo. "Still, it got us here."

But when it was time for Mr Koza to collect them, he phoned Gogo and said, "I'm very sorry, but my old car won't start."

"But I need to go back to school tomorrow!" cried Lolo when she heard the news.

"Don't worry," said Gogo, "I'll make a plan."

And the plan was to catch a lift with Mr Speedy, Aunty Boni's kind neighbour.

"But I can only take you halfway," said Mr Speedy.

Soon, they were cruising along the highway. Lolo smiled at Mr Speedy singing his happy songs to music on the radio. All the while, Gogo sat thinking of her next plan to get Lolo safely home.

"We'll have to hitch a lift," said Gogo
as they were dropped at the side of a busy
road. Lolo sat on her school bag and Gogo
stuck out her thumb.

A stream of cars sped by.

No one stopped.

"We'll *never* get home," sighed Lolo.

Then Gogo started waving her thumb
in the air and *that* did it! A minibus full
of singing people stopped, and there was
just enough space for Gogo and Lolo
to squeeze in.

"*Joy! Joy! Joy! We have joy in our hearts!*"
everyone sang.

Lolo felt happy – at last they were
going home!

But...

JOY!

somewhere along the way, the minibus turned off the highway and Gogo asked, "Where are we going?"

"To a church meeting in Crossroads," said a lady.

Oh dear! Crossroads was still far away from home.

"We'll have to catch a taxi," Gogo explained to a very tired Lolo.

It was easy to catch a taxi, but the taxi was
only going as far as a railway station.

Lolo and Gogo waited and waited. But
a train never came.

By this time, Lolo was floppy-tired and very, very hungry. So Gogo took her to a fruit market to buy some fruit. But when they got to the market, the stall keepers were all packed up. Poor Lolo sat down and cried... and cried... and cried.

"Why's your little girl crying?" asked a friendly fruit seller who was busy packing boxes onto the back of his donkey cart.

Gogo told him the WHOLE story.

"We'll never get home," wailed Lolo.

"Yes, you will," said the fruit seller. "I'm going past your home, so I can drop you off."

Gogo and Lolo sat in the donkey cart, eating some fruit that the kind fruit seller gave them to fill their hungry tummies.

The donkey cart moved slowly through back streets, but they were going in the right direction... *and they were going home!*

But...

just before they reached home, the donkey decided to stop and simply refused to go. "Here's fine, thank you. We can walk home from here," said Gogo.

And that's what they did.

Gogo was tired. Lolo was floppy-schloppy-tired.

"I've never *ever* been in a truck, a minibus, a taxi and on a donkey cart all in one day," said Gogo, dragging her bag behind her.

"Feet are best," yawned Lolo.

Gogo laughed. "You are right, Lolo. Feet never let you down!"

"Joy! Joy! Joy!" they sang as their feet
carried them the rest of the way home...

right up to their front door...

where Mama was waiting for them.

More Stories About Lolo

ISBN 978-1-91095-977-0

HOORAY FOR

LOLO

Niki Daly

ISBN 978-1-91095-969-5

Everyone Loves Lolo!

"Set in South Africa, this is a charming collection
of stories about the everyday adventures
of a young girl."
BookTrust

"Sparkly stories with lots of gentle humour
that will win Lolo lots of friends."
Red Reading Hub

"These sweet, simple stories are punctuated by
black and white drawings by the author.
The stories show how Lolo deals day-to-day
with life's little disappointments, learning good
manners and right from wrong, with the help
of her mother and Gogo, her grandmother."
Recommended Reads, Children's Books Ireland

Niki Daly

has won many awards for his work.
His groundbreaking *Not So Fast Songololo*, winner
of a US Parent's Choice Award, paved the way
for post-apartheid South African children's books.
Among his many books, *Once Upon a Time* was
an Honor Winner in the US Children's Africana
Book Awards and *Jamela's Dress* was chosen by the
ALA as a Notable Children's Book and by Booklist
as one of the Top 10 African American Picture Books
– it also won both the Children's Literature Choice
Award and the Parents' Choice Silver Award.
Niki wrote and illustrated the picture book
Surprise! Surprise! for Otter-Barry Books.
He lives with his wife, the author and illustrator
Jude Daly, in South Africa.